RUFF STUFF

SEARCH AND RESCUE COZY MYSTERIES, BOOK 2

PATTI BENNING

SUMMER PRESCOTT BOOKS PUBLISHING

Copyright 2024 Summer Prescott Books

All Rights Reserved. No part of this publication nor any of the information herein may be quoted from, nor reproduced, in any form, including but not limited to: printing, scanning, photocopying, or any other printed, digital, or audio formats, without prior express written consent of the copyright holder.

**This book is a work of fiction. Any similarities to persons, living or dead, places of business, or situations past or present, is completely unintentional.

CHAPTER ONE

"Oh, for me? You shouldn't have. This is the best birthday present ever."

Evelyn Foster accepted the teddy bear gratefully and smiled as she met the warm brown eyes of the one who had given it to her.

Atlas, her big, not-quite-two-year-old German Shepherd, cocked his head to the side and whined, his gaze darting between her face and the toy as if asking her what in the world she was doing and why she wasn't throwing it for him.

"Now that I think about it, I got this for you on your birthday last year, didn't I, buddy? It's rude to regift presents. I think you should take it back." She tossed the stuffed bear, and he snatched it out of the air, his tail wagging.

From the dog bed under the living room window, Willow, her nine-year-old sable German Shepherd, rolled over with a groan and gave the two of them an unimpressed look. Eve wrinkled her nose.

"Don't look at me like that, girl. Talking to my dogs is a perfectly normal thing to do."

Maybe pretending said dog was giving her a birthday present wasn't, but it wasn't like there was anyone here to judge her. Normally, Eve was content with her life. She had a job she liked, she got to work with her best friend every single day, and she had the best hobby in the whole world, not to mention two great dogs who made her life so much more full.

But on birthdays and holidays, sometimes she felt just a little … lonely.

While Atlas entertained himself with his stuffed bear and Willow tried to ignore him in favor of taking a nap, Eve checked her phone yet again, even though she knew she would have heard if it had gotten a notification. All she did was confirm that no one had sent her any happy birthday messages … and that she wasn't going to have time to stop at the coffee shop before work unless she left *right now.*

The thought of skipping her favorite morning treat on her *birthday* of all days was too much to bear, so she leaped to her feet.

"Atlas, come on, buddy. It's time to go to your room."

He was still young and rambunctious enough that she didn't want to leave him alone with the older and less tolerant Willow all day while she was at work, so she had turned her spare bedroom into a sort of dog room for him. There was a gate at the door, so he could still look out into the rest of the house while she was gone, and enough toys to keep him occupied all day.

Both dogs were used to their routine, so they didn't put up any fuss as she ushered Atlas into his room, gave them both treats, and headed out the door for work. She wouldn't say she *loved* working a nine-to-five job, but the regular schedule and guaranteed weekends off were a huge benefit in her opinion. Plus, working alongside her closest friend took some of the sting out of the forty-hour work week.

Getting a latte every morning took even more of the sting out of it. Yes, the copious amounts of sugar and coffee weren't good for her teeth, as her bosses liked to point out—Eve was a dental assistant, so those sorts of comments were part and parcel of her job—but she made an effort to have healthy habits in every other part of her life, and she wasn't about to give up one of her favorite parts of the morning.

As it turned out, the Granite Mug — the only coffee shop in the town of Granite, Michigan — offered a free breakfast pastry along with any coffee purchase if she could prove it was her birthday, so she left the coffee shop with an unexpected, and unexpectedly good, chocolate cheesecake muffin in addition to her usual iced latte this morning.

Things were looking up. As she walked from her car to the dental clinic's front door, she tried to focus on the positives instead of the fact that it was nearly nine and not a single member of her family had called or texted her with happy birthday wishes yet. She knew it was still early, and that she was maybe a little more sensitive about holidays and birthdays than other people, but if the whole day went by without a single birthday message from her family, it wouldn't be the first time.

She was adopted, and while her adoptive family always said she was just as much a part of the family as their blood relatives, it was the little things that proved them wrong. Most parents didn't forget their child's birthdays. And most children didn't have to be told that they were just as much a part of the family as everyone else—they just *were*.

"Happy Birthday, Eve!"

The ambush came as she was walking into the dental clinic. All Eve saw was a pink balloon and someone in even pinker scrubs before she was pulled into a hug that almost spilled her coffee.

"Thanks, Tiana," she mumbled into her friend's shoulder, squeezing her as tightly as she could with one hand holding her latte safely to the side.

She and Tiana had met at Northern Michigan University and had been best friends for the past decade and change. *Tiana* never forgot her birthday, and Eve made sure to return the favor whenever her friend's October birthday rolled around.

"So, I got you a balloon," her friend said as she pulled back. "And a card. I was going to get you a new pair of those hiking boots you like so much because I know you've been complaining about your old pair, but I didn't know what style you wanted so I just got you a gift card instead. Lunch is on me today, by the way. I already talked to mister Dr. Clark, and he said we can take as much time as we want, since it's your birthday and all."

The dental clinic they worked at was owned by a married couple, both of whom were dentists. Calling them both Dr. Clark got confusing sometimes, so Tiana and Eve had taken to calling them mister and missus Dr. Clark, depending on which one they were talking about.

Eve wasn't sure if either of them were aware of it, but she didn't think they would mind. They were both some of the nicest people she had ever met.

"Thanks, Tiana," she said with a laugh as she accepted her birthday balloon and card. "You're the best. You didn't have to get me anything, I'm just happy you remembered."

Her friend's face fell ever so slightly. "No messages yet?"

Eve shrugged, trying not to show how much it bothered her. "It's still early. And I know they're busy.

Plus, I've got you and a free muffin from the coffee shop, so I can hardly complain."

"Well, *after* work, I'm taking you out, all right? It's Friday and your birthday, and I'm not accepting any excuses. We'll go to Lake of Pints and see how many free drinks you can get when we tell everyone it's your birthday."

Eve grinned, torn between laughter and embarrassment. She had no doubt her very outgoing friend *would* try to get the whole bar to take part in her birthday celebration, but that wasn't her style.

"I'll go out with you for drinks, but I'm *not* accepting any free ones from strangers. Deal?"

Tiana gave a mock pout. "Deal. It's not as if I can argue with the birthday girl, is it?"

"You've got that right. Today is my day."

Even though she had to work, all in all, it was a good birthday. Mister Dr. Clark ushered her and Tiana out early for lunch and told them not to come back until one, so they spent the better part of an hour eating take-out sandwiches by the old lighthouse just to the east of town, along the Lake Superior coast. It was a gorgeous July day, without a cloud in the sky —

though there were plenty of seagulls clamoring for bits of their sandwich bread.

Eve ignored her silent phone and focused on what she *did* have; an amazing friend who went out of her way to make this day special for her because she knew Eve didn't have anyone else to do it, not really.

After leaving the dental clinic at five, they parted ways briefly to change and get ready for the evening. Eve let the dogs out back and spent a little while playing fetch with them.

"We'll do something fun this weekend, I promise," she said as she let them back in, both of them panting from the heat and exertion. "I know today's a boring day for the two of you, but I'll make it up tomorrow."

After changing into something a little nicer—Lake of Pints wasn't exactly a fancy pub, but it *was* her birthday—and touching up her makeup, she heard a honk out front and hurried out to get into Tiana's car. No driving for the birthday girl.

Lake of Pints was always busy on the weekends, so it wasn't surprising that they had to park a few blocks away and walk to it. Tiana seemed to be in high spirits and hurried ahead the last few steps to grab the door and pull it open for her.

"After you."

Smiling, Eve stepped into the pub and froze as a cheer went up from the corner.

Levi, Tiana's long-term boyfriend, was at the front of a group of people gathered by two tables pushed together. It only took Eve a split second to realize she recognized all of them; Aubrey and Elara, two mutual friends of hers and Tiana's from Marquette; Aidan and Alice, the cute guy she had met in the coffee shop a few weeks back and his sister; and Sophia, the woman who was letting Eve use her property to train her dogs, and who was becoming a good friend to her.

"What is this?" she asked, faltering in the doorway.

"Your party," Tiana said, beaming. "Surprise!"

CHAPTER TWO

"You didn't suspect? Not even a little?"

After a round of greetings, the group sat down around the two pushed together tables to order food. It was still early enough that the pub's kitchen was open, thankfully, because Eve subscribed to the belief that all food was magically calorie free on her birthday, which meant she didn't have to feel bad about the huge burger and plate of fries she ordered.

"Not at all," she said. She couldn't stop smiling. "You didn't let anything slip, Tiana. I didn't even know Levi was back in town."

Levi was a long-haul trucker and was sometimes gone for weeks at a time. He and Tiana had been together for five years now, and they made it work despite his schedule. Eve wasn't sure if *she* would be able to date someone who was gone so much, not that she was interested in dating right now anyway, but she was glad her friend was happy.

"He got back last night," Tiana admitted. "I'm pretty sure he slept all day today, but he was stoked for the party tonight." She lowered her voice. "I hope it's all right that I invited Aidan and Alice. I figured Sophia was a no-brainer, and Alice was there chatting with her when I stopped by to extend the invite, since I didn't have her number. Since they both know you, I thought it would be rude not to invite her and her brother along too. I tried to get Jan here too, but she's travelling for some dog thing this week. She said she'd call you this weekend, though."

Alice lived next door to Sophia's horse ranch and was good friends with the older woman. Aidan had recently moved to Granite and was currently staying with his sister. Eve didn't know what his long-term plans were. While she saw him a few mornings a week at the Granite Mug, since he was as much of a coffee fiend as she was, she had been trying not to let their chats get too deep.

She liked him. He was handsome, with his reddish-brown hair and eyes that looked either grey or green depending on the light. He seemed kind; she knew he had relocated to Granite so he could be there for his sister while she went through a tough divorce, and he was always polite to the employees at the coffee shop, even if they got his order or his name wrong. He tended to talk without thinking sometimes, but she even found that more cute than annoying.

In other words, she was in trouble. She didn't *want* to like him. She was done with dating. Maybe not forever, but her last breakup had gone badly enough that she wasn't eager to repeat the experience.

Yes, it had been over five years, but that didn't mean she was ready. Plus, she had a full life as it was. She was content. Why go out of her way to add what might turn out to be a hand grenade to her peaceful existence?

"Eve?"

"Yeah, sorry. It's fine, of course. It's nice that you invited them. They're nice people, and it's nice to have them here."

"That's a lot of 'nices,'" her friend murmured suspiciously. "You know, from how Aidan keeps glancing at you, I think he thinks you're *nice* too."

"Shut up," Eve whispered, feeling her cheeks turning red. Turning to Aubrey, she cleared her throat and raised her voice slightly. "I'm so glad you and Elara made it out! How have you been doing? Did you find a new job yet?"

As her friend responded, Eve did her best to focus on her instead of on Tiana, who kept wriggling her eyebrows and was silently trying to draw Eve's attention back to Aidan.

She loved Tiana, she really did, but sometimes she wished her friend didn't know her *quite* so well.

Despite the good-natured teasing, it was a lovely party. Sophia seemed a little down, but Eve understood why. Her husband's recent arrest had been hard on her, and running the ranch by herself was even harder. She boarded horses and gave riding lessons for a living, so she was constantly busy. Eve had taken to offering some help in the stable in exchange for Sophia letting her train Willow and Atlas on her property.

Sophia tried to turn her down, of course. Eve volunteered for Michigan Mutts Search and Aid, and Willow was an experienced search and rescue dog. Atlas was still in training as a cadaver dog, but she hoped he would be able to pass his final tests by the end of summer. Sophia assured her she was just glad to help, and Eve was using her old, empty barn and the trails through her woods for a good cause, but Eve knew how hard things were for her. She didn't mind mucking out a stall or two whenever she dropped by, even if she suspected that her company was more valuable to Sophia than the little bit of work she did.

Aubrey, Elara, and Tiana were all glad for a chance to catch up, and Levi just seemed happy to be doing something other than driving a truck. Alice mostly chatted with Sophia until Elara dragged her into a conversation about gardening. Eve hadn't even known Alice was interested in gardening.

Aidan chatted a bit with everyone, though he *did* seem to keep circling back around to her. She told herself it was probably just because it was her birthday. To be fair, *everyone* was a bit too focused on her. It was very heartwarming, and she was grateful Tiana had planned all of this. It went a long way to make her feel better about the fact that no one in her family had sent her so much as a happy birthday text yet, and it was after eight in the evening. Still, it got to be a bit much after a while, so she took a brief break under the excuse of going up to the bar to order another round of drinks for everyone.

She sat at a stool to wait for the bartender to make the drinks, and after a minute, she noticed that two guys a little further down the bar were watching her. They were younger, early twenties if she had to guess, and one was clearly whispering about her to the other. The one doing the whispering had curly blond hair and a camo jacket that was not at all out of place in a pub like this. The other one had dark hair, and frankly, looked like he might be homeless … though she wasn't sure Granite had a homeless population at all.

He was wearing a stained t-shirt with a torn sleeve, and when he rose to his feet, she saw that his jeans were torn too, in both knees. She knew torn jeans could be a fashion statement, but he looked like he had fallen and skinned both knees, tearing the jeans in the process rather than buying them that way.

She had never seen either of them before in her life and had no idea why they would be staring at her and talking about her, let alone why one of them was coming toward her with what could only be described as a terrified expression on his face. She might have been more worried if she wasn't in a crowded bar with her friends at a table just a few feet away.

"Can I help you?" she asked when he stopped a foot away from her and seemed to be trying to come up with something to say.

"Are you the woman with the dogs?" he asked. His voice was a hoarse whisper. "The dogs that find people, I mean? My friend says he's heard you talking about them."

She blinked. She supposed she did talk about her dogs a lot, and she and Tiana came here once a week most weeks, so it wasn't out of the question that someone might have overheard her and recognized her, especially since it was the only pub in such a small town. Still, it was a little weird to be *known* as the lady with the dogs who find people.

"That's me," she said after a moment's hesitation. "Sorry, who are you?"

"Michael. Um, Michael Baker. Here. Don't read it while people are watching."

He took another step forward and turned so his shoulder brushed hers. As he did, she felt him slip a folded piece of paper into her hand. Without another word, he walked away, and his friend got up to follow him out of the pub.

She blinked after them, then glanced down at the folded paper. A note. She had no idea what it was about or why he had given it to her, and she was about to unfold it when she hesitated.

He had asked her not to read it yet. Maybe he was just embarrassed about it, or maybe he had a good reason. Either way, it couldn't hurt to deal with it later.

It was her birthday party, and the bartender was walking over with a tray of drinks, and she was ready to rejoin her friends.

The mysterious note from the shady stranger would have to wait.

CHAPTER THREE

Eve didn't drink very much, which meant the three drinks she'd had the night before were enough to leave her feeling hazy and tired the next morning. The dogs woke her up, eager to be about their day, and after letting them out into the backyard, she cranked the hot water on in the bathroom and took a long, steamy shower.

She was pink skinned from the heat when she got out, but was feeling much better. When she returned to her bedroom to check her phone for notifications, her mood improved even more.

Happy Birthday, Eve! I'm so sorry I missed it yesterday, I've been swamped. I put your present in the mail on my way to work this morning. I hope you had a wonderful day.

The message was from her adoptive mother. Yes, it was a day late, but it still meant a lot to her. She typed out a quick response.

Thanks, Mom! Tiana set up a surprise party for me. I had a great time.

After sending the text, she bent over to pick up her clothes, which she had left in a heap on the floor when she changed into her pajamas after getting home late last night. Her black jeans were in a crumpled wad, and as she shook them out, something fell out of a pocket and onto the floor.

The note from the stranger. She had completely forgotten about it until now. Stooping, she picked it up and sat on the edge of her bed to unfold it. A scrap of fabric had been folded into it. Puzzled, she set the fabric to the side and read the note.

Please don't tell anyone about this. I think me and my brother's lives are in danger. My brother, Lucas Baker, is missing. We went camping Thursday night in the Granite Area State Forest, and we got separated. I made it back to town, but he didn't. I can't go into details because I don't want to put you in danger too, but something bad happened, and I'm worried about him. My friend says your dogs can find people. I cut a piece out of one of his shirts so they can get his scent. I drew a map of where we were when we lost each other. Please, find Lucas. Don't go to the police. Someone might be looking for us, and if our names are made public, he'll be able to find us.

That was it. The pleasant warmth from her shower had faded, leaving her feeling chilled. Or maybe that was just from reading the note, because outside, it was another hot, humid summer day.

The map that was scrawled beneath the note wasn't anything fancy, with a few lines labeled as roads and crude trees showing the forest. It wasn't much, but it was enough to give the search team an idea of where to start.

And the piece of fabric. Now that she knew what it was, she quickly got up and fetched a plastic bag from the kitchen to put it in, hoping it still held enough of the missing man's scent for the search dogs to use it to find him. Her mind was racing. She wished she had read the note yesterday, but she had completely forgotten about it by the time the evening was over.

Time was of the essence in cases like these. Thankfully, it was summer, so exposure to the elements wouldn't be a risk for Lucas, especially not at night, but there were still a lot of ways for a person to get injured or worse if they were lost in the woods and didn't know what they were doing. By now, Lucas would be hungry and thirsty, and if he drank water from the wrong source or stumbled across the wrong type of mushroom, he could make himself deathly sick without meaning to. If he was too injured or ill to call out, it would make finding him even harder.

She picked up her phone and wavered for a long moment, not sure if she should call the police or call the other volunteers at the search and rescue team first. The note had warned her against involving the police, but that in and of itself seemed like a sign that she should contact them. Whatever Lucas and Michael were involved in, it sounded dangerous.

And if it was dangerous, it wasn't something Michigan Mutts Search and Aid were prepared to deal with on their own.

Before she could decide, her phone rang, startling her. Tiana's name came up on the screen. She answered automatically, pressing the phone to her ear and giving a distracted greeting before she had time to wonder what she was doing.

She needed to figure out what to do about the note, not chat with her friend.

"Oh, good, you're up. I wasn't sure if I was going to wake you or not. How are you feeling? You didn't drink too much, did you? I know we don't usually go all out like that, but I figured we should have fun, since it was a special day."

Eve blinked, the familiar cadence of her friend's voice bringing her back to the moment, at least somewhat. Some of her panic ebbed, but she was still keenly aware of the clock that was ticking.

"Tiana, did you see a guy come up to me when I went up to the bar to get drinks last night?" she asked, launching right into the important stuff without preamble.

"Um, the kinda dirty looking guy you mean? Looked like he was barely old enough to legally drink?"

"Yeah, that's him. He slipped a note into my hand but asked me not to open it there. I forgot about it until this morning."

Tiana snorted, the sound feathery over the line. "I mean, kudos to the kid for shooting his shot. You should let him down easily. That takes courage. Though, it can't hurt to suggest that he cleans up a little before he tries passing notes to the next older woman he tries to pick up."

"I'm an older woman now that I'm thirty-two?" Eve squeaked, offended. Before Tiana could reply, she gave her head a rough shake. She was getting distracted. "Never mind. He wasn't flirting. The note was a plea for help. His brother is missing, and somehow, he knows I'm involved with search and rescue. He asked me not to go to the police, but I think I'm going to need to."

"Whoa," Tiana said, shifting gears instantly once she realized the seriousness of the situation. "That's a lot. How old's his brother?"

"The note didn't say." Eve's stomach twisted. "Gosh, I hope he's not a little kid. If he was, Michael probably would have gone to the police himself, right? I mean, even if he thinks someone's after him, he wouldn't just leave a kid in the woods alone all night, would he?"

"Hold on, the guy who gave you the note was named Michael?" Tiana asked, her voice tinged with something that put Eve immediately on edge. "Not Michael Baker, right?"

"That's right," Eve said slowly. "That's him. Do you know him?"

"No, I don't," her friend said. "But he was on the news this morning. Eve, Michael Baker was found murdered last night. That's what I was calling to tell you about. He was found beaten to death on a road just outside of town in the early hours of the morning. The news is all over town. It's all anyone's talking about."

"What?"

Stunned, Eve made her way into the living room and looked around for her laptop. Finding it on the coffee table buried under a magazine that advertised equipment and gear for working dogs, she sat down and opened it. After logging in, she searched *Michael Baker Granite Michigan* and waited for the results to load.

She clicked on the first link that came up. The article confirmed Tiana's story but didn't provide much more detail than her friend had. What it *did* provide was more information on Lucas. He was mentioned briefly at the end of the article.

Michael's brother, Lucas Baker, 21, is believed to be missing. If you are aware of his location, please contact the Granite Sheriff's Department at the number below.

Lucas was an adult, which was a relief, at least. He still needed to be found as quickly as possible, but the thought of some little kid lost out there had been horrifying to Eve.

Still, the news of what had happened to Michael turned her stomach. He had died only hours after giving her the note. She might have been the last person to speak to him besides the friend he had left with.

One thing was certain. There was no longer any question about involving the police. Michael had been right to worry about someone going after him, but keeping quiet about whatever was going on hadn't helped him in the slightest. Now his brother was out there, lost but still presumably alive, and Eve was determined to keep him that way.

"I've got to go, Tiana. I need to call this in to the police, and I'm sure they'll want Michigan Mutts on site as soon as possible." The sheriff in Granite was familiar with the volunteer organization and had worked with them in the past. She had no doubt her team would be involved in this. "I'll call you back when I know what's going on."

"All right," Tiana said, her voice concerned. "Be safe, Eve. Whatever these guys are involved in, it's bound to be dangerous."

CHAPTER FOUR

Volunteering with Michigan Mutts Search and Aid was a calling for Eve. She had her first experience with them back when she was twenty-five and a breakup with her ex, Adam, had left her lost and alone in the northern Michigan woods overnight. Being found by a friendly Labrador and his handler had been the turning point in her life.

As soon as she learned who the group that had saved her was, she knew she wanted to be involved. Michigan Mutts met as a group once a month, though its volunteers trained separately or in smaller groups a few times every week. She had started out just learning the ropes of search and rescue and getting certifications in things like first-aid and wilderness navigation. Then Willow's old owner, who had been a volunteer with Michigan Mutts at the time, got sick and had to find a new home for her dog. She had wanted Willow to go to someone who would keep doing search and rescue with her, and Eve had wanted her own dog by that point.

The rest was history.

Now, Willow was nine years old and nearing retirement, and Eve was a longstanding member of Michigan Mutts, fully capable of not only handling her own dog, but coordinating a search on her own. Everything snowballed after her phone call to the Granite Sheriff's Department. Sheriff Mary Larson had been skeptical but convinced enough to meet Eve at her house. One look at the note had been enough to convince her it was real.

Michael had left Eve the clues they needed to find his brother, and his death proved just how serious whoever else was looking for Lucas was. They were racing against the clock if they wanted to find Lucas alive.

Sheriff Larson's instant focus on finding Lucas let Eve know they were on the same page. She had no idea what Michael and Lucas were involved in, and at this point in time, it didn't matter. Finding him was what was important. Everything else could come after.

The sheriff recognized the area of the state forest the map indicated and told Eve to get a search party together as quickly as possible. "This is officially a missing person's case. I'd like to get this search off the ground within two hours. It's already almost noon, and the clock's ticking. Tell me what you need to get people and dogs on the ground, stat."

Eve had never actually organized a search on her own before, though she had helped Jan do so. It left her feeling both stressed and a little exhilarated as she made the calls she needed to make to get the other volunteers out to Granite.

Not all of them were close enough to make it in time, but between her, Jan, and two other members who lived within a couple of hours of the area, they had enough people to start a proper search of the area. It didn't matter to any of them what their other plans for the day were. They all knew what they were getting into when they started volunteering with Michigan Mutts.

Calls might come in few and far between, but when they did, it was always an emergency. A life was at stake, and that was more important than any weekend barbeque or beach trip.

"This is her second diving competition. I missed the first one because of work, and now I'm missing this one."

It didn't mean they couldn't complain, though. Heather, who handled a lovely redbone coonhound named Primrose—Prim for short—chatted as the four of them prepared their gear. Sheriff Larson had called in one of her deputies to supervise, and an ambulance waited at the turnoff they were all parked at just in case they were needed.

The Sheriff herself was presumably working on Michael's homicide case, though Eve hadn't asked. She was just glad the other woman was so quick to give her their official seal of approval. It made putting the search together a lot easier, and also gave them some legitimacy if they needed to cross onto private property. An examination of a map of the area told her that the state forest bordered a few private parcels of land around here.

"I'm sure your daughter will understand," Jan said. She was the de facto leader of this chapter of Michigan Mutts. The club's actual president was located in Sault Ste. Marie, and too far away to make it out here quickly. "It's just bad luck that you couldn't be there."

"My husband's recording it, but I still feel bad," Heather said with a sigh as she clipped the front strap of her backpack on. "I'm going to go get Prim out of the car."

Oliver, the fourth member of their group, was already waiting with his hound mix, Jackson. Jan had her own German Shepherd, a half-brother of Atlas's, and Eve had Willow with her. They were still expecting and hoping for a live find, so they didn't have any cadaver dogs with them at the moment.

Eve finished preparing her own gear and clipped her handheld radio to her belt. She hadn't been expecting to do this today, but then, she never was. None of them could predict when the call would come.

"All right, Willow. Are you ready to do this? Lucas is counting on us."

Willow knew exactly what they were doing. Eve could see the anticipation in her eyes, in the alert set of her ears and the way her muscles quivered as her wet nose scented the air. Even though she was getting older, Willow still lived for these searches, and Eve wasn't going to deprive her of it until she had to in order to keep her healthy.

As soon as they all had their gear and dogs in order, they had a brief conference with the deputy, made sure their watches and GPS units were all on and accurate, and then they headed out. Lucas could be anywhere by now, and in order to cover as much ground as possible, they split up. The sheriff's department had obtained more of Lucas's clothing from his apartment with a hasty search warrant, so they had more than enough material to give the dogs the scent.

Once they were a little way into the woods and near the location Michael had marked on his rough map, Eve opened the plastic bag she was carrying with the piece of Lucas's shirt in it and let Willow sniff the contents before she resealed the bag and tucked it into her backpack.

"Ready, girl? Search."

Willow led the way, and Eve followed. A dog's nose was a marvelous thing and gave them access to a world of scent that was completely alien to humans, but it wasn't magical. It couldn't pick up a smell that wasn't there. If Michael's information was wrong or the wind was uncooperative, they might spend hours out here without any luck. Eve was prepared to wander around the woods for however long it took, or at least until dark, when the teams would have to retreat for their own safety.

Thankfully, it didn't take that long. After only twenty minutes, Willow's body language changed. She raised her head and scented the air, then started pulling toward the north. Eve's pace quickened as she followed the dog, not quite jogging because the undergrowth didn't allow for it, but moving faster than a walk.

It was a hilly area, though thankfully it had been dry enough out lately that the valleys between the hills weren't as muddy as they usually were. Still, it was hot work, and Eve was about to call for a break to get both of them some water when she crested the hill they had been working on and nearly had a heart attack when she saw a man sitting not even twenty feet away on a log.

Her first thought, with a burst of hope, was that he was Lucas Baker, the very man they were looking for. She knew she was wrong as soon as the thought had crossed her mind. Lucas was a twenty-one-year-old young man with brown hair and ears that stuck out to the sides. The deputy had brought a picture of him along with his clothes.

This man had brown hair, but that was where the similarities ended. He looked to be in his forties, and had a thick beard covering his jaw. He was wearing the sort of tweed hat she had only ever seen on older men and held a pair of binoculars in his hand and was giving her a vaguely annoyed look.

Willow gave him a cursory, curious look, then tugged the leash in the direction they had been going, eager to be on their way.

"Wait, girl," Eve said. She slipped the leash's end loop around her wrist before slinging her backpack off and unzipping it to get out the copy of Lucas's photo she had been given.

"Pardon me, miss, but would you mind moving on with your dog? You've frightened away a pair of grey catbirds. I'm hopeful they might come back when you leave."

Eve blinked. "A pair of what?"

"Gray catbirds are small, grey birds which make vocalizations that sound like the meowing of a cat." He must have seen the sheer skepticism on her face, because he added, "They're very real, I assure you. My name is Joeseph Carlson, and I'm the president of the local birdwatcher's club."

For all she liked nature, Eve had never gotten further into bird identification than the basics. She knew the differences between a robin, a blue jay, and a crow, and the other common species, but had no idea if this man was pulling her leg or not. It didn't really matter; she was here to find Lucas.

"Sorry for disturbing you, Joeseph," she said. "My name is Eve, and this is Willow, and I'm with Michigan Mutts Search and Aid. We're taking part in the search for a missing person, and we are looking for this man." She handed him the photo. "Have you seen him?"

Joeseph examined the photo closely. "Sorry, miss, I can't say that I have. I did see what looked like the remnants of a camping site a few hundred yards that way." He pointed in the direction Willow had been leading them. "But it was on the other side of some private property markers. The man who lives there is notorious for chasing off trespassers, which is a shame because he has some *very* rare nesting pairs on his property."

"Thanks," Eve said as she accepted the photo back from him. "That's helpful information. If you *do* see Lucas, please be aware that he has been missing for over twenty-four hours and may be disoriented, confused, and frightened. There is a deputy waiting at the Lime Road turnoff with an ambulance. Hold on, I can get you a card with the sheriff department's number—"

He shook his head and stood up with a sigh, slipping his binoculars into his pocket. "If there's a whole search going on, it sounds like I'm not going to get any peace. I might as well head home. I hope you find this man alive and well. Good luck."

"Oookay," Eve said quietly as Joeseph strode away down the hill. She felt a little stung that he was so clearly annoyed by the interruption. It wasn't like she was ruining his birdwatching on purpose—they were looking for a missing person. It was important!

She slipped the photo back into her backpack and gave Willow a chance to sniff the bag of Lucas's clothes again before they set off.

Joeseph might not have been the friendliest person, but he *had* given her useful information about the campsite. She didn't know yet whether it was relevant to the search or not, but she *did* know Willow was heading right toward it.

CHAPTER FIVE

It only took them another minute or two of walking before she spotted the signs of a campsite through the trees and smelled the scent of stale smoke. Someone had been here recently, within the last forty-eight hours, and this was right around the area Michael had referenced on his crude map. She didn't want to get too excited, but her gut told her it had to be Michael and Lucas's campsite.

Unfortunately, Joeseph had been right when he said it was on the other side of a private property line, and the line was posted, with purple signs nailed to the trees every few feet. Whoever owned this property clearly was just as unfriendly to trespassers as Joeseph had said.

That didn't stop Eve. The campsite was *right there*, and Willow was clearly interested in investigating it. If someone asked her to leave, she would, but if Lucas was injured or confused for some reason, there was no reason to believe he had wandered onto public land instead of private land.

"All right, hold on, girl," Eve said as they crossed the invisible boundary and approached the campsite. It was just a few feet on the other side of the property line. She wondered if Michael and Lucas had trespassed on purpose or had somehow missed the signs.

It was definitely a recent campsite. There was a fire pit, which had since gone cold, but the ashes hadn't blown away or been rained on yet. A small tent was still set up, and there was a pot of congealed food next to the fire pit, as if whoever had been here had left in a hurry.

"Lucas?" Eve called out, wondering if he had circled back around and returned to the campsite at some point. He didn't answer, but she approached the tent anyway. "Lucas, if you're in there, please come out. I'm Eve, and I've got my dog, Willow, with me. We're with Michigan Mutts Search and Aid, and we're looking for you. People are worried about you."

Still no response. She reached slowly for the tent flap and was about to pull it open when a branch snapped with a sound like a gunshot. Jolting, she twisted around at the same time Willow let out a single, sharp bark. The dog immediately looked chagrined, since she knew she wasn't supposed to bark at people in public like this, and especially not when she was working, but it was clear the man who was standing about ten feet away had startled both of them.

"What do you think you're doing here?" he snapped. He had grey hair and was wearing a camouflage t-shirt and khaki shorts with hiking boots. An empty garbage bag hung from one hand. "This is *my* property. I don't know how many more signs I have to put up to make it clear."

"Sorry," Eve said, feeling immediately on the defensive. "My name is Eve, and I'm looking for—"

"I don't care if you're looking for bigfoot! Get off my property!"

He took a step closer, and Willow grumbled uncertainly, her instincts fighting against her training. Eve rested a soothing hand on the dog's back.

"Sir," she said, trying to force some authority into her voice. "I'm with a search and rescue team looking for a missing person. I will leave your property, but I would like to show you his picture and check this tent first. I believe he and his brother camped here at some point recently."

The man's cheeks were red with anger by this point, but he finally looked at Willow's bright orange vest that had the words *Search Dog* embroidered on it and the equipment hooked to Eve's belt, and seemed to realize she wasn't the average trespasser. He gave the tiniest, incremental nod and gestured at the tent.

"Don't think there's anyone in there, but go ahead and look. I found this campsite yesterday morning and it was already abandoned then. Probably some kids doing drugs. They're lucky they didn't burn down the whole forest. Foolish kids, starting fires in the middle of a dry forest without so much as clearing the area around it first…"

While he grumbled, Eve quickly crouched down and peeked into the tent. There were two sleeping bags and a rucksack, but it was empty other than that. She straightened up.

"You're right, it's empty. You didn't see the people who were camping here?"

"You can bet your bottom dollar that if I *did*, I would have run them off. Now I've got to clean up the trash they left behind. I'm too old to be doing this. Kids don't have any respect these days."

She glanced at the trash bag in his hand. It was one of the big, black, heavy-duty ones. "Wait, are you saying you're going to throw the tent and their other belongings away?"

"What else do you expect me to do? Donate them to charity? I'm not going to leave all of this junk sitting out here, littering the forest."

Eve took a deep breath and tried to see things from his perspective. Yes, it probably was annoying to have to deal with trespassers coming onto his property from the state forest. It sounded like Michael and Lucas's campsite wasn't the first problem he'd had to deal with. And if he didn't know that Michael was murdered and Lucas was missing, then he had no reason to think the tent and their belongings were anything other than junk some kids had left behind.

He was rude and aggressive, but he probably had very valid reasons to be annoyed.

"I'm sorry, Mister… I just realized I never got your name. I'm Eve Foster, and this is Willow."

"Connor Evans," he grunted.

"Well, I'm sorry, Mister Evans." He seemed like he would appreciate her being as respectful as possible. "I understand how frustrating this must be. I did see your no trespassing signs, and I do feel bad for ignoring them, but my dog is trained to find people by following their scent, and she followed the scent of the missing man, Lucas Baker, right to this campsite. I'm thinking she was probably following an old scent, but I had to be sure. We'll be out of your hair in a jiffy, but first, can I show you a picture of the man we're looking for?"

He crossed his arms. "Fine. Get on with it."

She quickly took the picture out of her backpack and handed it over. He glanced at it, then handed it back.

"Never seen him before in my life. Is he some sort of criminal?"

"Not at all," she said. "He's lost out here. We're just trying to find him and help him. We've got a deputy and an ambulance waiting back at the Lime Road turnoff."

He grunted. "Well, he's not here. You want to search my property, you're welcome to, assuming you get that deputy to show me a search warrant. Otherwise, scram."

Right. Not helpful at all. At least he wasn't yelling anymore.

"One more thing," she said as she zipped her backpack back up. "It might be best if you don't move the tent and their other stuff quite yet. The police might want to look through it."

He just grunted again and crossed his arms, clearly waiting for her to go. She sighed and clicked her tongue to Willow. They would have to go back to public land and follow the property line, hoping Lucas had wandered back into the state forest at some point and they could pick his trail up again.

She waited until she was out of earshot and off Connor's land before she unclipped the radio at her waist. She had to report what she found and let the others know the landowner was being uncooperative. Maybe the deputy could talk to him and convince him to let a search team onto his property.

Before she could press the call button, her radio crackled to life.

"This is Team Prim," Heather said. "Code Green. I repeat, Code Green. We're heading back to the rendezvous point now."

Relief burst in Eve's chest. Code Green meant that Heather and Primrose had found Lucas alive and without any major injuries.

"Let's head back, Willow," she said, patting her dog. "You did a good job, but Prim found him this time."

She would still report the campsite, but it could wait until she got back. Finding Lucas had been the important thing.

Now they just had to get him back to town and figure out who was going to break the news about his brother.

CHAPTER SIX

"He's a little dehydrated, but otherwise all right," Heather told the rest of them. They were huddled near their vehicles while the paramedics looked over Lucas and the deputy spoke to him.

"Where'd you find him?" Jan asked.

Heather unfolded a topographic map of the area—they all had one for each of the counties in Michigan's Upper Peninsula—and indicated a spot about a mile northwest of where Eve and Willow had found the campsite.

They probably *would* have found him, if Heather hadn't gotten there first. Willow had been on the right track. Eve sent a warm smile at the dog where she was waiting in the car, her head poking through the open window. Eve had given her a bowl of water and a toy to chew on, but the dog was more interested in what they were doing.

No matter how many searches they went on, Eve never stopped feeling proud of Willow.

"Where was that campsite you said you found, Eve?" Jan asked.

Eve pulled herself out of her thoughts and found the coordinates on the map. "Here. It was on private property, but only by a few feet. I had a conversation with the owner. He was … unpleasant."

"Hopefully, someone from the sheriff's department can go get his things," Jan said. Her eyes fixed on something over Eve's shoulder. "Speaking of, it looks like the deputy's done talking to Lucas."

Eve turned. Sure enough, the deputy was on his way over to their little huddle. A man by the name of Victor Hubble, she didn't know much about him other than that he had been Sheriff Larson's deputy for half a decade. He certainly looked the part; in fact, with his brown, brimmed hat and the sheriff's deputy patch embroidered on his jacket, he looked like he could have stepped out of a movie.

"I'd like to thank you again on behalf of Sheriff Larson for your help," he said. "It's always good to find a missing person alive and well. Unfortunately, it sounds like we've got another problem. He didn't say anything to you about why he and his brother left their camp so late at night and got separated?"

That last sentence was directed toward Heather, who shook her head. "He didn't talk much at all, other than to answer my questions about whether he was injured and if he was able to walk back to the rendezvous point with me. I didn't want to chat too much, because, well, I was afraid the topic of his brother would come up, and I sure didn't want to be the one to break the news to him."

Deputy Hubble grimaced. "Don't blame you for that. It's the worst part of the job, at least for me. Anyway, he says he and his brother fled because someone threatened them with a gun after they saw something they weren't supposed to." He gave them a serious, somber look. "They saw this person burying a body."

Eve's eyes widened, and she exchanged a look with the others. Jan cleared her throat. "Has anyone else been reported missing?"

"I radioed in to check. Nothing high-profile, but there is a man, Logan Young, about the same age as Lucas and his brother, whose boss called in a welfare check on him this morning because he hadn't been in to work for a couple of days. Our other deputy went to check it out, and he wasn't at his apartment, but there wasn't any sign of a struggle, and his car was gone, so it's possible he left of his own accord."

"I found what I believe to be Lucas and Michael's campsite," Eve said, her mind racing. "I was just telling the others. It was on private property, but only a few feet over the property line. A guy named Connor Evans practically chased me off, but their things were still there when I left."

Deputy Hubble sighed. "Yeah, I know Connor. We've had to deal with a lot of calls from him."

"Is he a known criminal?" Heather asked, looking worried.

The deputy snorted. "No. He was the one doing the calling. He's well known around the department for trespassing people at the drop of a hat. He's called in to complain about people turning around in his driveway, even just walking down the road in front of his house too often. As far as I know, he hasn't ever threatened anyone with a gun, but I wouldn't put it past him."

"Do you think he killed someone for going onto his property?" Eve asked, her eyes wide. She hadn't thought she and Willow were in real danger out there, but if Connor killed a man…

"He's never been violent in all the time I've known him, but he's getting older. People snap." He shrugged. "I'll go check it out. You didn't happen to see anything incriminating while you were talking with him, did you? No half-buried bodies on his side of the property line?"

"No, I didn't see anything." Not that she had been looking. If she'd had Atlas with her, maybe things would have been different.

"Well, according to the kid, it was dark out when all this happened. You want to know my thoughts, it's that there wasn't a body at all. Connor probably came out and tried to scare them off his land, the kids got spooked and ran, and Lucas here built the whole thing up in his head after being lost in the woods for a day and a half. I'll go check it out anyway, but I wouldn't be surprised if that other kid, Logan, turns up after the weekend and this all turns out to be nothing."

"Well, what about Michael?" Eve asked. "Someone killed *him*."

Deputy Hubble frowned. "The sheriff's working on his case, but as far as I know, there isn't any evidence that what happened to him is connected at all. It's sad, of course, but as far as Granite has a bad part of town, these two young men come from it. A lot of young people out here don't have much to do besides drugs and getting into trouble. Sometimes that comes back around to bite them. I don't want any of you to worry about it too much. You already helped, and we're grateful to you for that. If the sheriff has any questions for you, she'll get in touch. Right now, you are all free to go."

"Thank you," Heather said. "I've got to get home and see how my daughter's competition went."

"Do you think it'd be all right if I spoke to Lucas before I go?" Eve asked the deputy.

She could understand why he wanted to assume that Lucas's warning meant nothing, and they didn't have a second murder to deal with, but it still sat wrong with her. She had given the note to Sheriff Larson, and she doubted the deputy had the time to read it yet, but Michael had clearly been scared in it. She fully believed that he and his brother had seen something more frightening than an angry old man waving a gun around.

"I don't see why not," he said. "Don't take too long, though. He declined to go to the hospital, so the paramedics can't take him. That leaves me to drive him back to town, and the sooner I can get that over with, the better. I've got a lot of paperwork to do if I want to clock out at a reasonable time."

"I could drive him."

The words were out almost before she had a chance to think about them, but she didn't regret the offer. It would give her a chance to talk to Lucas about Michael. Even if the deputy was right and there hadn't been a second murder, she was sure Lucas would want to hear about how determined Michael had been to find him. It might hurt, but in the years to come, she suspected the knowledge of his brother's last evening would be a balm to him.

Deputy Hubble gave her a slow blink, then glanced back toward where Lucas was waiting by the ambulance. He shrugged.

"I don't see why that wouldn't be fine. It'd save me some time, and he seems like the type who wouldn't like riding along with a deputy very much anyway. As long as he doesn't have any objections to it, I don't. The sheriff's going to want to meet with him, but she gave me the all clear to drop him off at his apartment first, so he can get cleaned up and get some food in him. She'll swing by his place in an hour or two to see what he knows about his brother."

Eve nodded and went over to Lucas with the deputy at her heels to arrange his ride. He didn't seem to care much either way who he rode with, though when he saw Willow with her head out the window of Eve's station wagon, that seemed to sway him enough to accept her offer.

"So, do you like dogs?" Eve asked as they walked toward her vehicle.

She felt a little awkward now that she had gotten what she wanted. Lucas had been lost in the woods for a day and a half and had just found out his brother had been murdered. He had to be reeling.

The younger man nodded slightly, his gaze far away as he stopped to pet Willow through the window. "Yeah. We had a German Sheherd mix growing up. He went on all sorts of adventures with me and Michael."

He clenched his jaw shut at the mention of his brother and opened the passenger door to get into the vehicle. She walked around to the driver's side and buckled herself in before starting the engine.

"I'll be honest with you, Lucas, I offered to drive you because I wanted to talk to you about your brother. But if it's too painful for you right now, it can wait."

He shook his head. "No, what is it? Do you know who killed him?"

"I'm sorry, but I don't. I think I might have been one of the last people who spoke to him before he was killed, though. He found me in the pub last night…"

She told him all about Michael and the note, and her own efforts to get a search team out to look for him this morning. Lucas listened intently as she spoke.

When she was done, he said, "That means you believe me, right? About the body? I could tell that deputy didn't. But if Michael was that scared, you've got to believe what we saw was real."

She bit her lip as she drove, thinking. Did she believe them? She certainly didn't think Lucas was *lying*, but it sounded like it had been a frightening situation, and she knew how the mind could play tricks on people.

But both him and Michael seemed convinced that something bad had happened out there, something worse than a grumpy old man threatening to shoot them for trespassing. And Michael had been *scared*. He had thought someone might be after him … and had been killed just hours after giving her the note. She couldn't shake the feeling that his death was tied to whatever he and Lucas had seen.

"I believe you," she said. "There's another missing man in town. His name is Logan Young, and Deputy Hubble said he's about your age. Do you know him?"

Lucas's eyes widened. "Yeah, I know Logan. He went to high school with my brother. They were friends. Not close friends, but they hung out sometimes."

There was no doubt left in her mind that all of this was connected somehow. She had a terrible feeling that Logan really was missing, and they weren't going to find him alive. "Please don't take this as me saying your brother was a criminal or anything like that, but do you know what he and Logan were involved in? I'm new to Granite, but I can't imagine what could lead to two murders happening in the same week."

"I never really hung out with them," he said. "So I don't know what they were doing. Michael wasn't doing drugs, though. I know that much. He was all about making money and saving up to move somewhere with more going on."

"Do you know anyone who might know?" Eve asked. "He was with someone at the bar last night, a guy with curly blond hair and a camo jacket. They left together, and they seemed like friends."

"That's got to be Mason," Lucas said. "If anyone knows whether Michael and Logan were involved with anything shady, it would be him. He was Michael's best friend."

CHAPTER SEVEN

She and Lucas exchanged numbers before she dropped him off at his apartment. It felt bad, leaving him alone after so much happened, but she didn't know him well enough to offer to keep him company, and he assured her that he would be all right.

He had seemed exhausted when he got into the vehicle with her, but now he had a new fire in his eyes. Eve still hoped that the sheriff's department would start looking for a body when Logan didn't show up to work after the weekend was over, but until then, it seemed like she was the only one on Lucas's side. Maybe if they found evidence that Logan really was missing, or that he and Michael had been involved in something dangerous together, then Sheriff Larson would be able to do something.

Right now, the only lead she had was Mason's full name and the place he worked. Lucas hadn't known his number off the top of his head, and his phone was one of the many items he and Michael had left behind at the campsite. Still, it couldn't be too hard to find him. He worked at the convenience store that was connected to the biggest gas station in town. There couldn't be more than one Mason Bailey working there. All she had to do was figure out what shift he worked and show up.

She called the convenience store after she got home. She was sitting on her patio, Atlas and Willow romping through the yard together as the call rang. Normally, she wouldn't expect a stranger to give her information about what shifts someone worked, so she was prepared with what she hoped was a convincing argument. It seemed like a clearly bad idea to give out that sort of information—what if she was a stalker, or had some sort of grudge against Mason?

As it turned out, not everyone felt that way. The girl who answered the phone either didn't like Mason that much, or didn't get paid enough to care, because when Eve asked when his next shift was, she said, "He'll be in this evening. Gets here at six for the evening shift. Anything else I can help you with?"

"No, thanks. That was it."

A little stunned, but also relieved at how easy the information was to get, Eve politely ended the conversation and checked the time. It was just before five. She had plenty of time to shower and try to organize her thoughts before she went to the convenience store and talked to Mason.

It didn't escape her attention that Mason, being the last person who anyone was certain was with Michael, might be involved in his death. Going to talk to him could be dangerous, but talking to him while he was at work, with other people around, should negate most of the risk she was putting herself in.

Unless he tracked her down later. She reminded herself not to forget that he somehow knew who she was, at least, enough to tell Michael she had search dogs. Yes, she talked about the dogs and Michigan Mutts enough that it could be something he had just picked up by overhearing her while she was at the pub with Tiana, but it was a good reminder that nothing was secret in a town this small … not even personal information like her address or her hobbies.

But … he was Michael's friend. Michael had gone to *him*, and not anyone else, for help when his brother was missing. If anyone knew the details about what Michael saw that night in the forest, or who or what he might have been involved in to lead to his murder, it was Mason.

She knew that, without a body, it was hard for the police to begin a homicide investigation. But she didn't need that much evidence to believe Lucas. She just needed a way to convince the rest of the world that Michael's murder wasn't the only one that had taken place in Granite recently.

After a lazy hour of resting and scrubbing herself clean of the long romp through the state forest with Willow—which included checking both herself and her dog for ticks, since the nasty parasites were all over the place up here—she gave both dogs toys filled with frozen peanut butter and yogurt and headed out to the convenience store.

The drive didn't take her long, but it was long enough that she had time to worry about what she was doing. The sensible part of her said that she should leave well enough alone. She had done her part. She had found Lucas. It was up to Sheriff Larson and her deputies to do the rest.

But Michael had given that note to *her*. She was involved whether she wanted to be or not, and her heart told her that trying to figure out the truth might not be the safe thing to do, but it was the *right* thing to do.

She had stopped at the joint gas station and convenience store perhaps a dozen times since moving to Granite. There was a second, smaller gas station in town, but the prices here were better. Never before did she have to build herself up to going in, but this time, she spent a few minutes just sitting in her car, going over what she wanted to say and ask and trying to convince herself that sticking her nose into this mystery wasn't going to end up with *her* being the next victim.

Finally, she had to force herself to just do it. Taking a deep breath, she got out of her car and strode the few steps under the hot summer sun to the building's entrance. It was cooler inside, and there was another customer browsing the drinks section. Mason was standing behind the counter, idly scrolling on his phone.

He looked up a second after she came in, and she knew the moment he recognized her because his eyebrows went up and he set his cell phone down.

"Hi," she said, still feeling nervous as she approached the counter. "I'm Eve. Your friend, Michael, handed me a note asking me to help find his brother last night."

"I remember," he said flatly.

This close, she could see the dark circles under his eyes, and it made her realize with a jolt that *his friend had been murdered.* He had probably only found out this morning. If he *wasn't* involved in Michael's death, then this was probably one of the worst days of his life.

"I'm sorry," she said, suddenly backpedaling. "I shouldn't have come here. I'm so sorry for your loss."

He gave a sharp shake of his head as she started to turn away. "Stop. Sam told me someone called asking when I'd be in. I guess that was you. You're here for a reason, something about Michael, right? Or about Lucas? Did you find him?"

Of course. He didn't know Lucas was all right. It had only been about two and a half hours since they found him, and it wasn't as if the police would have a reason to let him know Lucas had been found. Lucas himself had a lot to deal with right now, and it probably wouldn't have occurred to him to contact Mason either.

"Lucas is fine," she said. "Michigan Mutts Search and Aid found him a couple of hours ago. He was lost and a little dehydrated, but otherwise unhurt."

The relief on Mason's face seemed genuine, though it was tinged with regret. "Good. Michael would have been… He would have been glad. He and Lucas didn't always get along, but they were still brothers, you know?"

"I could tell how important it was to him that someone helped Lucas when he slipped me the note last night." She took a deep breath. She still felt terrible that she hadn't stopped to think about what Mason was feeling after all of this, but she was already here. "I wanted to talk to you. Is now a good time?"

He shrugged and looked around the little convenience store. "It's not like we're busy."

"Right. Well, first, do you know why Lucas and Michael were camping out there? You said they didn't always get along, so I'm guessing they didn't camp together often."

"Thursday was Lucas's twenty-first birthday," Mason explained. "Michael felt bad because their dad took him out to drink on his twenty-first birthday, but he isn't around anymore, and Lucas didn't have anyone else to celebrate with. He thought going on a camping trip with a bunch of alcohol with his brother would be a fun way to celebrate his birthday. Their dad used to take them both camping a lot, so it was a nostalgic sort of thing, I guess."

Eve's heart sank. "It was Lucas's birthday? Wow. I had no idea. That makes it all so much worse."

"There's not really anything that could make what happened to Michael *better*."

"That's true. Did he tell you anything about what happened when he and Lucas got separated? They went camping Thursday night, but he didn't give me that note until Friday night, and frankly, he looked like he'd just crawled out of the woods. Was he out there that whole time?"

"From what he said, he got turned around after he and Lucas were separated. At some point he realized he was just getting more lost in the dark, so he hunkered down out there for the rest of the night. In the morning, he found his way back to the road, but he was miles away from where he had parked. He got back to his car sometime in the afternoon and started looking for Lucas when he realized his brother wasn't there. I guess he did that for a few hours, because it was evening when he showed up at my house and told me his brother was missing."

"You didn't try to get him to go to the police?"

Mason snorted. "I did, actually. He was adamant that it was too risky. He didn't want to draw attention to them. He told me he and Lucas saw someone burying a body out there in the woods, and he was worried that if the person learned who they were, he'd come after them. I honestly didn't know what to think, but I remembered there was a woman who I'd seen at Lake of Pints a few times who kept talking about her search and rescue dogs."

He nodded at her. Eve felt her cheeks turn pink. Did she really talk about her dogs that much?

He continued, "I suggested we go see if we could find you or anyone who knew who you were and ask if you could help without contacting the police. He was really paranoid, though. I've never seen him like that. I thought he was having some sort of mental breakdown or something. I guess he was right to be worried, though."

"What happened after the two of you left?"

He snorted. "You sound just like that sheriff when she talked to me earlier. Like I told her, we left the pub, and I offered for him to come back to my place to get cleaned up, then I'd go back out in the woods to help him keep looking for Lucas tomorrow. He said he wanted to get back to his place. His car was still at my place, but he said he was going to walk and try to clear his head. Letting him walk away last night was the worst mistake I've ever made."

Mason didn't seem like a killer to her. He seemed genuinely sad for his friend. She couldn't even begin to imagine the guilt he must be feeling.

"I'm sorry," she said again. "I know talking about this can't be easy."

He shrugged. "You found Lucas. I figure Michael owes you—and since he isn't here, I owe you for him. You must be asking all of these questions for a reason."

"I am. I believe what Lucas told me about seeing someone burying a body, but I don't know how much the police are going to be able to do without evidence. I'm trying to help. What happened to Michael has to be connected to what he and Lucas saw … unless Michael was involved with, I don't know, a gang or drugs or something dangerous."

Mason snorted. "A gang in Granite? You're joking. And Michael wasn't involved in hard drugs or anything criminal. We'd both seen enough friends ruin their lives that way to not want anything to do with it. No, you're right to think his murder is connected to what they saw. I wish I could tell you more. He said it was too dark to see the person clearly, but he was certain it was a man, and they brandished a shotgun or a rifle at him and Lucas. He didn't get a good look at the body either. I tried looking online to see if there were any missing people in the area, but I couldn't find anything."

"There is one," she said. "Though I'm not sure if he's an official missing person yet. Logan Young. Do you know him?"

His eyes widened. "I do. He hung out with us sometimes. We all went to high school together."

That confirmed what Lucas had said, at least. "Was *he* involved in anything that might have led to his murder?"

"No way. He was a hard worker, always doing odd jobs for people. He took care of his grandmother, so he didn't have much time to get in trouble." He frowned. "Actually, there was one thing. A couple of weeks ago, someone robbed his grandmother's house."

Her eyebrows twitched up involuntarily. "She was *robbed?* Did they file a report with the police?"

"Yep. Nothing ever came of it, though. Whoever did it cleared out all of her valuables. She was one of those people who bought stuff she never used. I went over there once, and she had a bunch of those unopened as-seen-on-TV boxes in her living room. I guess whoever cleared her place out took *everything*. Logan was pretty mad someone would target an old lady like that, but as far as I know, he never figured out who did it."

"If he *did* figure it out, do you think he would have confronted the person?"

"Definitely. He was *mad*. If he landed himself in trouble somehow, then my guess would be it had something to do with that. And if he's missing like you said, then his body might be the one Michael and Lucas saw." He shook his head. "Darn. I can't believe Logan is gone too. Too many people I went to school with have died."

Eve's mind was spinning. It all had to be connected. If they found whoever robbed Logan's grandmother, it might lead them to the person who killed both Logan and Michael. But if the police hadn't been able to figure out who robbed her, how could she?

CHAPTER EIGHT

It was well into the evening by the time Eve got home. Talking to Mason had been both helpful and frustrating. She was now more convinced than ever that someone here in Granite was responsible for two murders but finding them seemed harder than ever.

All she could do was find lost people. Finding stolen items was going to be a lot more complicated.

It had been a long day, and she felt like her thoughts were going in circles, so when she got home, she decided that she had done enough for today. She jotted a few notes down in her phone, then decided to think about it more tomorrow. Right now, she was both mentally and physically exhausted, had more than a few itchy bug bites, and hadn't eaten anything besides a few granola bars she had brought with her on the search earlier that day.

She didn't know if she could solve this mystery on a full stomach, let alone an empty one.

Not thinking about something was harder than it seemed like it ought to be, but she gave it her best that night. Tiana wanted an update and details, of course, but Eve got her to agree to wait until tomorrow. They decided to meet for brunch. Hopefully, two minds would be better than one, and Tiana would have some ideas after Eve laid everything out for her.

In the morning, she took the dogs on a walk around her neighborhood first thing, right after her coffee, since she wasn't sure what the day would bring, and she didn't want them to be completely bored if she ended up not coming home until the evening again. After freshening up, she left to go meet Tiana at Superior Slices, the little sandwich shop and deli right across from the dental office they worked at, for brunch.

When they met at the restaurant, Tiana chatted about how her own day had gone as they ordered their food, but Eve could tell from the looks her friend kept giving her that she was going to get the third degree as soon as they sat down. Sure enough, once they had their order numbers and had claimed a table, Tiana dove right in.

"The last thing I heard, other than the text you sent last night to let me know you found the guy, was that a recently murdered man slipped you a note right before his death asking you to find his missing brother. Girl, I need the details. What exactly *happened?*"

Eve launched into her explanation, glad for the chance to talk to someone she trusted, someone she knew beyond a shadow of a doubt wasn't involved in any of this. Tiana was a good listener, nodding every so often and only interrupting if she needed something to be clarified. When she finished, her friend looked a little overwhelmed—which was exactly how Eve felt.

"Well, that's it. That's why I went MIA yesterday. I didn't get a chance to thank you for my birthday celebration, so I'll do that now. I had a wonderful time Friday night, Tiana, and I really appreciate that you put the evening together for me."

"You don't have to thank me," Tiana said, though she looked tense. "It *was* a fun evening. I'm sorry things went so sideways yesterday morning, though I'm glad you found that missing man alive. I can't imagine how panicked he must have been when he realized he was well and truly lost."

"I can," Eve said with a grimace. Her friend reached across the table and squeezed her hand in sympathy. With a brief, grateful smile, she added, "I can't imagine what he must be feeling right now, though. Getting rescued, only to find out his brother was *murdered* while he was missing? I feel terrible for him."

"Is that why you're so determined to figure out what's going on? I'm not saying I blame you—thinking about a killer having free reign here in Granite with no one the wiser gives me the shivers."

"I guess I feel a little responsible," she replied after a moment's thought. "Michael gave *me* the note. I wasn't the last person to see him alive, but it was close. If I'd read it right away, things might have turned out differently for him. I know it's not my *fault*, exactly. He did ask me not to read it where anyone could see, and of course I had no reason to think it was a matter of life and death, but to a certain extent, things turned out the way they did because of my actions."

"I'm just worried you're going to put yourself in danger," Tiana said. "If you believe Lucas about the body he said he and his brother saw, then that's two people this person has already killed. There's no reason to think he will stop there if he thinks his secret is at risk of getting out."

"I know," Eve said. "I *do* believe him, and I'm well aware of how dangerous this person is. It's not like I'm planning on chasing him down and making a citizen's arrest. I just want to find some solid evidence of what happened. Considering where Lucas and Michael were camping, there's a good chance the body was buried somewhere on private property, which means the sheriff would need a search warrant to look for it."

"Oh, yeah, you told me about that angry guy who chased you and Willow off. It's his property, right? Doesn't that make him the obvious suspect."

"He's certainly ornery enough," Eve muttered. "He *did* say he had been having a lot of trouble with trespassers, though. His land is posted, but there's no fence, so anyone can walk right onto it. I don't want to make assumptions without knowing more. Plus, I think whatever happened to Logan has something to do with the burglary at his grandmother's house. I don't know how that would tie back to Connor."

"I remember hearing about a string of thefts a few months back," Tiana mused. "I don't think they ever found out who was behind it."

"I just wish we could find the body. Without a body, it's hard for the police to determine that there's been a homicide. Once they know for sure there's been a second murder, they can really kick things into gear, and I'll be happy to sit back and follow their progress online from the safety of my house."

Tiana bit the inside of her cheek. Eve knew the expression well; her friend wanted to say something but wasn't sure it was a good idea. Finally, she came out with it.

"I'm just thinking, the *police* need a warrant to search private property, but you don't. You do have an almost fully trained cadaver dog. If you were, say, out on a walk with him and he just happened to pull you onto that man's property and alerted that he found something, it's unlikely you'd get in trouble, right? You're a civilian, so it's not like whatever evidence you found would be inadmissible in court just because you didn't go through proper channels. I'm not saying you *should* do that, because that man very well might be a killer twice over and it would be about the dumbest thing ever to walk onto his property looking for a dead body ... but hypothetically, you *could*, right?"

"I'd still be trespassing, hypothetically speaking."

"It's not like you'd be going out there to damage his property or steal anything," Tiana said. "Atlas can pick up scents from a good distance away, right? So if you walk him along the property line on the public side and he doesn't smell anything, well, you haven't done anything wrong. If he *does* smell something, I think you've got a pretty decent excuse for checking it out."

Eve bit her lip. If she could find the body Lucas and Michael had seen on Thursday night, it could be what the police needed to blow the case wide open. On the other hand, she wasn't sure how she felt about side-stepping the law like that. Though, now that she thought about it, there might be a better way.

"You know what, I bet Lucas wants his camping equipment back," Eve said. "And I know Connor

Evans wants it off his property too, if he didn't already throw it away. If I can get Lucas to come with me, we can just nip out into the woods to get his things, and we'd be doing Connor a favor by taking the tent and all their other stuff away. Atlas can come along for company, and if he happens to alert on something while we're there, you're right. I'd be duty bound to see what he found."

"I'm going to regret this, aren't I?" Tiana said with a sigh. "You'd better text me when you go out there, and if I don't hear back from you, I'm going to go right down to the sheriff's department and tell them they'd better get out there to save you before you get murdered too."

It was a dangerous plan, and a questionably legal one at best, but Eve knew it was the only way forward. She didn't have to follow the same red tape the police did, and she had something that the little Granite Sheriff's Department didn't.

A dog who was trained to find bodies.

CHAPTER NINE

Despite Eve's newfound resolve to find the evidence of a second murder on her own, she was equally resolved to be as careful as possible, which meant only going if Lucas would go with her. There was safety in numbers, and an extra set of eyes and ears couldn't hurt.

She was certain Lucas would want to help her find the body and proof that he was telling the truth about what he and Michael saw, and when she called him that afternoon, he proved her right by jumping at the chance ... but even though she was raring to go, there was an unforeseen stumbling block.

He was spending the day with his parents.

"I can try to leave in a couple of hours, but they're going to worry," he said over the line. "I think they need me, after what happened to Michael. We're all taking it pretty hard."

"No, no, you should stay," she said quickly. "Going back out into the woods can wait for a day or two. Spending time with your family is important."

"Tomorrow?" he asked. "My boss gave me the week off of work after hearing about what happened. I could meet you anytime."

"It would have to be after five," she said. "I could probably pick you up around five-thirty or six, which would leave us with a few hours of daylight. It should be enough time."

He hesitated. "You'll be able to find your way back to the car, right? Even if it starts getting dark while we're out there?"

She heard the fear in his voice and understood why he was so worried. He had probably grown up running around these woods without a care in the world, never believing he would get seriously lost in them. Now that it had happened, he likely didn't trust his own sense of direction anymore and would be terrified of a repeat occurrence.

"I have a map of the area, and I'll bring a spare compass for you," she said. "I also have a GPS locator if the map isn't enough. Don't worry. I promise, we won't get lost out there."

They solidified their plans for the next day, which left her at something of a loose end for today. Tiana was planning on spending the day with Levi, since he was only home temporarily, and she didn't know anyone else in town well enough to just send a text and ask if they wanted to hang out. She probably could ask Alice or Aidan, but it would be awkward at first, and she knew she would be distracted the whole time thinking of the murders and worrying about everything that might go wrong tomorrow.

She liked both siblings and they seemed like decent people, but she wasn't sure she knew them well enough to tell them about everything that was going on like she had with Tiana.

Training the dogs was always an option, but she had spent half the day yesterday out in the woods and was looking at doing the same thing tomorrow, so it didn't exactly sound like an appealing option right now. All that left for her to do was run some errands and then get some chores done at home.

With a sigh, she pulled away from the curb in front of the sandwich shop and turned toward the grocery store … or what passed as a grocery store in a town as small as Granite.

Braggie's Best General Store sold just about anything anyone could want, as long as what they wanted wasn't fresh produce or meat that hadn't been frozen for years. Not having a real grocery store in town was a drag, but Eve was beginning to get used to having to drive half an hour to Marquette for fresh food, and the little general store was starting to grow on her.

Shopping there was always an experience. The shelves were packed from floor to ceiling, with everything from tools and hardware, to canned and dry goods, to clothing and pet supplies. There was a frozen goods section and a refrigerated section that provided a few basics like eggs and milk, and an entire wall dedicated to locally made goods: jerky, honey, bread, and pastries.

Eve never went shopping without a list, but whenever she went to Braggie's Best, her list seemed to go out the window, and she found herself putting things she hadn't known she needed into her basket.

The aisles were too narrow for carts.

It was still the weekend, which meant the little general store was busier than it usually was during the week. She shuffled through the aisles, occasionally backtracking to let someone else by, and tried to focus on buying only what she needed rather than whatever caught her eye.

Normally, she passed right by the as-seen-on-tv section, but after hearing Mason's story about his grandmother being robbed, she stopped to browse this time. She felt bad for his grandmother, she really did, but if this was the sort of stuff that had been taken, maybe she was better off without it. A lot of this stuff was *weird* and seemed questionable at best and a straight up scam at worst.

Though … there was a mini heat sealer that was only five bucks. She took the box off the shelf to look at it, skeptical but almost willing to risk wasting the five dollars on it. How convenient would it be to be able to reseal bags of chips or dog treats after she opened them?

"Don't bother," a man said from behind her left shoulder. "I've got one of those at home. It worked well … for about the first thirty seconds. Now it barely gets warm enough to heat the plastic up a few degrees."

She turned and was shocked to come face to face with Joeseph Carlson, the birdwatcher she had run into in the forest yesterday. He seemed to recognize her too, because his eyebrows rose in surprise.

"Thanks," she said, putting the mini heat sealer back on the shelf. "I always thought most of these were scams anyway."

"Some of them are decent. That salad spinner, for example." he said, nodding at the box on the shelf. "My wife swears by it."

"Too bad they don't sell salad to go along with it."

He let out a huff of laughter. "If they did, it would be three times the price as it is anywhere else. This place really hikes the price tags up over what you can find in a supermarket. I never really noticed until I lost my job a few months back, then let me tell you, driving half an hour to shop in Marquette seemed a lot more appealing."

"I guess they can charge whatever they want, since there isn't any competition in town."

"You're right about that. Listen, Miss, I should apologize for being short with you when you were looking for that young man a couple of days ago. It seems like whenever I find a good spot, someone comes along and wrecks it, but that isn't your fault. If you asked me a few years ago whether more people spending time outside in natural spaces was a good thing, I would have said yes, but I suppose the reality is it makes it harder to find quiet areas for birdwatching and hunting like I used to be able to. I've been trying to work on my temper for a while now. I know I can be a little short with people when I'm interrupted, so I'm sorry. I really am."

"Don't worry about it," she said. He nodded farewell and turned to go, but an idea occurred to her. "Wait. You're out there a lot, right?"

He nodded. "Yes. Nearly every day. Not always in the same area, but once I know where the nests are or where feeding areas are, I like to return on a rotation to check up on the birds. They have amazingly complex lives."

Birdwatching was one of those hobbies she had always heard about, but never met anyone who actually *did* it until now. Joeseph certainly seemed passionate about it, but that wasn't what she needed to know right now.

"You didn't see anyone walking around with a shovel and a gun last week, did you?"

He raised one eyebrow. "I can't say that I did, no. Just the normal hikers."

"Right. Thanks."

She sighed as he left and glanced back toward the as-seen-on-TV items. The truth was, she didn't eat enough salad to need a salad spinner. She liked her vegetables just fine, but not in leaf form. Give her a nice, roasted zucchini or some raw broccoli and dipping sauce over iceberg lettuce and romaine hearts any day.

CHAPTER TEN

Bright and early Monday morning, Eve got a call from the sheriff.

"Good morning, Ms. Foster. I hope I didn't wake you. I was trying to catch you before work."

"I've been up for a while," Eve said. It was a few minutes after eight; she would have to leave soon if she wanted to get a coffee before she went to the dental clinic. "I'm just sitting outside while the dogs play. You can just call me Eve, by the way."

"Well, we might be seeing a fair amount of each other if the last few weeks are anything to go by. You've certainly got a knack for turning the town on its head."

"Well, I'm not doing it on purpose," Eve said.

Sheriff Larson chuckled. "I know. I just wanted to touch base, eh, see if there's anything else you can remember from when you were out looking for Lucas and found that campsite. I heard from my deputy that you drove him home. Could you give me your perspective on how he seemed while he was in the car?"

A little puzzled, Eve gave the other woman a summary of what she and Lucas had discussed—and added in her conversation with Mason for good measure.

"Thank you. Mason Bailey did get in touch with us to share some of the ideas the two of you came up with. We're looking into all avenues right now, and we're waiting for a call from Logan Young's workplace to see if he turns up to work today or not. Right now, I'm just trying to cover all my bases."

"You don't think there's any way Connor Evans would let you on his property to look for evidence of what Michael and Lucas said they saw?" Eve asked, hopeful. Maybe she and Lucas wouldn't have to go through with their plan this evening after all. It sounded like the police were taking this seriously.

The sheriff snorted. "Oh, I know Connor. He'd be hollering at us to get off his property before we even reach his door. No, we're going to need a valid warrant to step one foot on his property in any sort of official capacity."

"Do you think he's behind all of this?" Eve asked, biting her lip as soon as the question was out. The sheriff probably couldn't tell her much.

Sure enough, Sheriff Larson said, "Well, I'm not going to speculate. But I do know Connor hates guns. He doesn't own one, doesn't let hunters on his property with them, and thinks they're the devil's work. And Lucas is adamant that he and his brother were threatened with a gun. Plus, while Connor's a little persnickety about his privacy, we have answered a number of valid trespassing calls from him over the years. It's something he has to deal with a lot, since the property backs up to state land right by a popular turnoff. Make of that what you will, but I hope you won't speculate too much either. This is a small town, and people are already scared enough with Michael Baker's murder. If it turns out we really do have a second homicide, things are going to get bad, fast. I don't want anyone pointing fingers at anyone else without some rock-solid evidence."

"I understand," Eve said, her mind racing. "Thanks, sheriff. Sorry I couldn't be more helpful."

They said their goodbyes and Eve ended the call, then got up and called the dogs in so she could finish getting ready for work.

She had really been thinking Connor Evans was behind everything. It made sense. He was quick to anger, hated trespassers, and, well, that was it, really. She had no idea how he could be connected to Logan's death, but for all she believed that Lucas wasn't making things up … it had been dark. Maybe he and Michael *had* been mistaken about what they saw, and Logan would show up to work today like nothing had happened.

But he couldn't have threatened Lucas and Michael with a gun if he didn't *have* a gun.

She turned the problem over in her mind while she was working that day, but he was really the only suspect she had. Well, there was Mason, but why would he have killed his own friend? That didn't make any sense either.

Eve had to remind herself that she wasn't out to solve a murder. She just wanted to prove beyond a doubt that there had been one.

Usually, she chatted with Tiana for a few minutes after work, but today, she hurried on her way so she could let the dogs out, grab her gear, and then go pick Lucas up. She promised Tiana that she would text her when they went into the woods and when they came out, and her friend promised that if it was past dark and she still hadn't heard from her, she would call in the calvary.

Eve really hoped it wouldn't come to that.

Atlas was thrilled to get into the car with her, and doubly so when he saw all of their gear. He probably thought they were going to train. She hoped he wouldn't pick up on how nervous she was—it could affect how well he did his job. He was still in training and didn't have the confidence that Willow did.

Lucas was waiting outside his apartment building when she pulled up and got into the passenger seat after briefly saying hello to Atlas, who gave him a cursory sniff before looking at Eve as if to ask what this stranger was doing with them.

They were both tense as she drove them out of town and up to the section of state forest he and Michael had been camping on. Whatever the outcome of today was, it wouldn't be a good one, and they both knew it.

CHAPTER ELEVEN

"So, why were you and Michael camping on Connor's property, anyway?" Eve asked.

They had been walking through the woods for a few minutes. Atlas wasn't searching yet—she wanted to wait until they got a little closer to the location of the campsite—but he clearly knew they were out there for business and was on exceptionally good behavior.

"Who's Connor?" Lucas asked.

He was clutching the compass she had given him like his life depended on it, and if she had to guess, a good part of the strain on his face had nothing to do with the fact that they were out here looking for a body, and everything to do with being back out in the woods after spending more than a day hopelessly lost out here.

"Connor Evans. The landowner whose property you were camping on."

He gave her a blank look. "As far as I know, we were camping on public land. We didn't have a map, though. If it wasn't posted, we'd have no idea where the public land ended and the private land began."

"It *was* posted," she said. "You'll see, he has signs up every few yards."

Sure enough, when they reached the area near where she had found the campsite, the purple *Posted* signs were still up all along Connor's property line. Lucas frowned when she showed him.

"I'm turned around already. Are you sure we're in the right spot?"

"Positive."

"We didn't set up camp until after dark. We must have missed the signs. It was hard to see anything in the dark. We didn't mean to trespass, though."

"Well, we're here," Eve said. "Let's get started. This guy really hates people going on his property without permission, so we should be careful not to cross the boundary unless Atlas smells something. How close to the campsite were you when you found the person burying the body?"

"I don't know. Far enough we couldn't see the fire. We'd gone out to find some more dry wood. We only had one light between the two of us, and with how thick all this undergrowth is, we didn't see the guy until we practically stumbled over him and the body. It all happened so fast. We saw the body, the guy shouted and waved his gun at us, and we took off running. We got separated a few minutes later, and I never managed to find the campsite again … or my brother."

It had just taken an instant for everything to go wrong. She gave him a sympathetic look before reaching down to unclip Atlas's leash from his collar and reattach it to his harness.

"All right, buddy. You know what we're out here for. Search."

Atlas took the lead, though he wasn't pulling toward a scent quite yet. As they walked, Eve made sure to keep them on the public side of the property line, though they followed it toward where the campsite had been. Since Lucas didn't know where exactly they had seen the man burying the body, maybe they would get lucky and find it here on the land that they had a legal right to be on.

If she could consider finding a body lucky at all.

She called Atlas to a halt when they reached an area she recognized. "This is where the campsite was." She frowned. "It looks like he cleared all of your stuff out. I wonder if he gave it to the police, or if he just threw it away."

Lucas grimaced. "We really did miss those signs. I recognize this place. You're right, this is where we were camping."

He hesitated, then crossed over the property line. Eve followed him, glancing around to make sure Connor wasn't lurking behind a tree somewhere. She really didn't want to run into him again if she could help it.

All of the items, including the tent, had been removed, but they found the charred remnants of the campfire scattered through the leaves. She was eager to continue on with their search, but Lucas had a lost expression on his face as he gazed down at the blackened sticks. She decided to let him have his moment.

Maybe the wind changed ever so slightly, or maybe Atlas just turned his head the right way at the right time, but she could tell the exact instant he caught a scent. His body went taut, his ears pricked up, and he started pulling strongly in a certain direction, farther onto Connor's property ... and farther away from the state forest.

"Lucas, he has something," she said urgently.

He tore his attention away from the remnants of the campsite and looked at the dog. "Let's follow him. Hurry."

She let Atlas lead the way, her heart pounding as they shoved through the underbrush. This was his second real find, and the first intentional one. A part of her was dreading what they were about to uncover. Not for the first time, she second-guessed her decision to train him to be a cadaver dog.

When it came down to it, she really didn't like finding dead bodies.

She could tell they were getting closer when he began to pull at the leash with more intensity and began to whine almost constantly as he tugged her forward through the trees. Suddenly, he stopped and sniffed a patch of leaves that looked disturbed even to her own inexpert eyes.

He sat abruptly and let out a single bark. She winced —when she trained his alert, she hadn't been expecting them to go on covert finds like this.

"Let's see what you found, buddy."

She took her backpack off and unzipped it to remove the hand trowel she had packed and put on a pair of latex gloves so she wouldn't inadvertently mess up what might be a crime scene.

"I don't know," Lucas said, looking around. "I don't think this is the right place. I'm pretty sure we headed downhill from the campsite to look for wood. This is uphill, and it's the wrong direction."

"I trust my dog," she said.

Telling Atlas to stay, she dropped his leash and kneeled in the dirt. After brushing the layer of leaves aside with her hands, she carefully began digging with the trowel.

It only took a few seconds before she felt something that wasn't dirt beneath the trowel's blade. She used her gloved hands to clear the dirt away.

Lucas let out a surprised grunt as she uncovered a patch of pale skin, then a face. Her own stomach roiled, but she clenched her teeth. They had found what they were looking for.

"It's Logan," Lucas muttered. "I think I'm going to be sick. I swear, this isn't where we saw the man burying the body."

"Whoever buried his body must have moved it after you and Michael stumbled across it," she said. Carefully, she brushed a layer of leaves over Logan's face. "We have our evidence. It's time to bring in the authorities."

After moving a careful distance away from the body, she took Atlas's favorite tug toy out of her backpack. "Good job, buddy! You did it."

His tail wagging, he bounded forward and took one end of the toy in his mouth, tugging it hard enough to nearly make her stumble.

"What are you doing?" Lucas asked, shocked.

"He needs to be rewarded for his find," she said with a grimace, though she kept tugging on the toy for Atlas. "If every time he finds a body, everyone gets upset, he's not going to have any reason to want to keep searching. Think of it as his payment for a job well done."

Lucas shook his head, but refocused on the patch of leaves under which the body was hidden. "What now?" He pulled his phone out of his pocket to check the screen. "There's no phone service out here."

"We'll go back to the car. We had service there, so as soon as we get close enough, we'll call the police." And she could text Tiana to let her friend know that she hadn't been murdered.

"We can't just leave him out here. Someone already moved him once. What if they come back and see that the ground is disturbed? They might move the body again."

"I don't think it's safe for one of us to stay here alone."

"Please," he said. "Logan's death is one more clue about what happened to Michael. Someone murdered my brother, and I need to know why. This is the only proof we have that something more is going on than what looks like a random attack otherwise."

Biting her lip, Eve went back and forth in her mind for a few moments before giving in. "Fine. I'll stay here with Atlas. You go to the car and call the sheriff's department."

His eyes widened. "I should stay. I can't get back on my own."

"Lucas, you have my compass. I'll give you the map. It's a twenty-minute walk if you hurry. You can do it. It makes more sense for me to stay out here, since I'll have my dog with me. He's a big dog, and he'll be a good deterrent if the killer does come back. Plus, he gives me a good excuse for why I'm out here if Connor sees us. I'll just say I dropped his leash and he ran off and I had to come get him or something. If he sees *you* out here, it's going to be a much bigger issue."

He still looked uncertain, but accepted the map from her nonetheless. She showed him what direction to go, made sure he knew how to use the compass, then watched him walk away until the undergrowth swallowed him.

Despite her assurances, she wasn't as confident as she wanted to be that he would be able to find his way back to the car quickly. It was an easy walk, she hadn't been lying, but he looked on the verge of panic, and panic could lead even the smartest people to making dumb mistakes.

CHAPTER TWELVE

Eve decided not to wait right next to the body. Not only would it be obvious what she had found if the killer came back to check up on the shallow grave, but every minute she and Atlas were there, they ran the risk of disturbing or destroying hidden evidence.

After putting everything back into her backpack, she and Atlas moved closer to the property line, but still close enough to the body that she would be able to hear if someone else approached the area. She found a log to sit on and settled in to wait.

Seconds turned into minutes, and eventually she took out her phone and started making a grocery list for the next time she went to Marquette and could stock up on produce. It felt almost absurdly mundane given the circumstances, but what else was she supposed to do? Sit here and stare at the trees for an hour or more?

She vaguely registered the crunching of leaves, but it took Atlas suddenly sitting up and cocking his head to make her realize that what she was hearing were footsteps. Hurriedly, she slipped her phone into her pocket and stood up. She was about halfway down a small hill, and the footsteps were coming from the other side of it—the side that was closer to public land, back the way Lucas had gone to reach the car.

It was way too soon for him to be coming back with the police, so unless he had gotten turned around, that meant a stranger was headed her way.

"Keep quiet, Atlas," she whispered. She rose to her feet and, moving with as much care and silence as possible, crept up the hill with Atlas beside her. Just before she reached the top, she told him to lie down and peeked over the ridge herself.

Joeseph Carlson, the birdwatcher, was on the other side.

He had his binoculars to his face and was looking up at a tree, but as she watched, he lowered them briefly to glance around, a shifty look on his face. She was hidden enough that he didn't see her, and a moment later, he returned to watching the tree with his binoculars. Far above, she spotted a few little birds playing in the branches.

There was no doubt in her mind that he knew he was trespassing. She remembered him talking about some rare nesting pairs on Connor's property. It seemed that he was determined to check on them regardless of the fact that they were on private land.

Before she risked him seeing her, she crept back down the hill to where Atlas was waiting and grabbed his leash. She really didn't want to talk to Joeseph right now. He would wonder what she was doing out here, and she didn't know whether to tell the truth or come up with a lie.

Moving slowly and carefully so as not to make a lot of noise, she led Atlas further down the hill and away from the birdwatcher, heading back towards the body. Joeseph had chosen a terrible time to sneak onto Connor's land, but she would leave him to it and would just have to hope that his birds didn't lead him toward where Logan was buried.

It was an unfortunate coincidence … if it was a coincidence at all. Frowning, she wondered just who Joeseph *was*. She knew he liked birdwatching, but that was about it. Well, that, and the fact that he had a wife who liked an as-seen-on-TV salad spinner.

Not even ten feet from where the body was hidden, she froze. The as-seen-on-TV stuff. She didn't know anyone personally who actually *bought* that sort of stuff. What she *did* know was that a bunch of it had been stolen from Logan's grandmother. There was no evidence tying the theft to the murders, but it was kind of a big coincidence, wasn't it?

Someone stole a bunch of as-seen-on-TV items from an elderly lady, leaving her grandson mad and ready to confront whoever was behind the theft. That same grandson whose body she and Atlas had just found. Hidden on Connor's property, yes, but Connor didn't own a gun, at least according to the sheriff.

When she spoke to him at the general store, Joeseph had mentioned he hunted in addition to birdwatching. If he hunted, then chances were he had a gun. And Joeseph had some of those as-seen-on-TV items she had been looking at, but where had they come from?

The general store, or a phone order … or maybe stolen out of a little old lady's home?

Joeseph had lost his job a few months ago, which was right around when those robberies Tiana had mentioned started. It seemed absurd to think that the man was behind a string of thefts, but now that she thought about it, he had the perfect setup, didn't he?

He was a birdwatcher. It was the perfect excuse to sit somewhere with binoculars and watch the world go by. Watch *people* go by, and maybe even figure out their schedules and know the best time to break into their homes.

Atlas tore her from her thoughts by pulling on his leash. He was trying to get back to where Logan was buried. He seemed confused, and she couldn't blame him since they never just hung around the area after a find. He probably thought he was supposed to find the scent again.

She stopped walking. "No, buddy. We're done. We're hiding now."

He whined, unsure. She shook her head and turned away, looking around to try to figure out where she should wait or what she should do. It didn't feel safe out here anymore, and she wanted to let Lucas and Sheriff Larson know what she had realized.

Then Atlas barked.

CHAPTER THIRTEEN

It was a single bark, born out of his impatience and uncertainty. He wanted to go do the thing he was trained to do—find the body. He didn't understand why she was just standing there, not doing anything.

But it didn't matter *why* he barked, not really. What mattered was that he did, and that Joeseph heard it.

It only took a few seconds for her to hear the man's footsteps as he hurried toward their location. Adrenaline and panic zinged through Eve's body as her mind raced. She could bluff, maybe, pretend she was out here chasing after Atlas like she had planned to do if Connor saw them, but she didn't think she would be able to pull it off. She was too scared, and Joeseph was bound to notice.

Frozen in fear and indecision, she ran out of time. Joeseph shoved his way past a spindly pine tree and paused when he saw her and Atlas. His brows furrowed as his gaze lingered first on Atlas's bright orange vest that had a patch reading *Search Dog* on it, then on the recently disturbed patch of leaves Logan was buried under.

There could be no doubt in his mind why she was there. At least his gun wasn't on him today. The only thing he was armed with was a pair of binoculars.

And she had a big dog. She'd bet on Atlas over some binoculars any day.

"Hi," she said, trying not to wince at how high and nervous her voice was. "Nice day, isn't it?"

"I keep running into you," he said, his eyes darting between her and where the body was buried. "What are you doing out here?"

She couldn't figure out whether it was better to tell the truth about finding the body and not let on that she knew he was the killer, or to play dumb about everything. Her silence must have lasted a beat too long, because he took a step closer to her as if to pressure her into a response.

Atlas made a low grumbling sound that wasn't quite a growl. Joeseph paused.

"Did your search dog find something?"

He seemed to be making an effort to keep his tone casual. She took a deep breath and tried to do the same.

"Look, um, this isn't the best time. I'm here on official business. It might be best if you left the area for today." She tried to give him a polite smile, but she knew in her gut it was coming off as nervous. "We found the body of a missing man. My partner has contacted the police. They're on their way now."

"Your partner? You mean that kid who passed me by on his way back to the turnoff?" He glanced back the way he had come from, a dangerous glint in his eye. "He looked a little lost. If you want, I'll go make sure he found his way out of the forest. You can just wait here with the body."

The truth was, she didn't know how far Lucas had gotten. He might not have even reached an area with cell service yet, or he might be on the phone with the sheriff as they spoke. What she *did* know was that if

Joeseph went after him, Lucas would be in very real danger.

Joeseph didn't know that she suspected him. He might think he would have time to go silence Lucas, then return to do the same to her. Lucas, however, wasn't aware of the danger.

"Wait!" she said as Joeseph turned to go. "I know what you did."

He froze. Her heart was pounding in her chest, but she told herself this was the right choice. Lucas would be defenseless if Joeseph confronted him right now. He didn't even know to be wary of the man. While she doubted she would be able to fight Joeseph off if it was just her, she had the benefit of having a big dog on her side.

Slowly, he turned back to her. "Do you, now."

"I just want to know why," she said. "I lied, I'm not out here with anyone else. Atlas and I found the body on our own. I know someone who knew Logan, and he told me about the burglary at his grandmother's house. All the as-seen-on-TV stuff she was collecting. Then when I talked to you at the general store yesterday, I put two and two together. You're behind the thefts, aren't you? Did he confront you or something? I mean…" She hesitated. Maybe she could convince him she was on his side. "Was it self-defense? No one would blame you for that."

He paused, seeming to consider her words. She tried to look curious instead of terrified out of her wits. She wasn't sure how well it was working.

"Do you have any idea what it's like to be the breadwinner for your family, and then lose your job?" he asked after a moment. "The despair? The embarrassment? I never in my life thought I could feel so low."

She nodded slowly, as if she understood. "That's why you started stealing? To make ends meet?"

"I had plenty of time on my hands all of a sudden, and for the first time, I realized how much *excess* some people had. It started with scrap metal. A whole pile of the stuff someone was letting go to rust, when all they had to do was haul it in. Then a garage full of empty cans, some years old, that no one was returning. These people weren't *using* any of this stuff. That old lady I took those as-seen-on-TV items from? Half her living room was stacked full of unopened boxes. I'm not a bad guy. I was only taking things people didn't need, and I used the money I got from selling all of it to pay my bills and support my wife until I found a new job."

"I mean, that's understandable," she said. She even meant it, to an extent. She could see how desperation could drive someone to what they thought were petty thefts. "How did it get to murder?"

He glanced at where the body was buried than shook his head roughly. "I don't even know." He sounded tired all of a sudden. "I was washing my car in my driveway. I'd left the garage door open, and I still had some of those as-seen-on-TV boxes stacked against the back wall. Out of the blue, some kid in his twenties came at me accusing me of stealing from his grandma. He must have seen the boxes when he was passing by. He attacked me first. He *did.* I thought he was going to kill me. I grabbed a tire iron and did what I had to do to defend myself."

The confession sat heavily in the air between them. It took her a moment to find the words to ask her next question. "Why didn't you go to the police?"

He gave her a look like she was crazy. "Because there would be no hiding that I stole all of that stuff. Self-defense or not, I'd have ended up behind bars for theft. My wife didn't know. The conviction would have ruined my marriage, heck, my entire life."

"Then why bury him here? On private land, instead of in the state forest?"

He crossed his arms and wouldn't quite meet her eyes as he muttered, "I figured this way, if someone found his body, the landowner would get blamed. Maybe he'd go to prison, or have to move, and I'd be able to talk whoever lived here next into letting me use this part of the property for birdwatching."

"You tried to frame a man for murder because of ... birdwatching?"

He actually looked embarrassed. "I was already in too deep to worry about right and wrong. Turned out to be the worst mistake I'd made in a while, anyway."

"Because of Michael?"

"I'm not confessing anything else," he said. "I'm just trying to make you understand. I'm not a danger to anyone else. You don't have to call this in. The man I killed, he attacked me first. The only thing I did wrong was hide the body. Well, and steal some things, but I'm done with all of that now."

"But it's not the only thing you did," she pressed. "You killed Michael too, didn't you? If I *do* keep this secret, how do I know my body won't be the next one they find on the side of the road."

She had no intentions of keeping his secret, of course, but if she could make him believe that she might until Lucas and the sheriff arrived, that was all that mattered.

"I wasn't thinking when I went after him," he said. "I saw him walking alone late at night. I was driving past, on my way home from work. I met his eyes through the window, and I just *knew* he recognized me. I thought killing him was the only way to keep him quiet. Do you think I've been sleeping well? Beating two men to death with a tire iron isn't something I want on my conscience. I'm not going to add more to that burden if I don't have to."

She shuddered but tried to play it off by reaching down to pat Atlas's head. "I see. Well, you don't have to worry about me. I'll keep my mouth shut and I'll just—"

"I knew it! Sheriff, there's two of 'em there, including that girl with her dog. I told you I heard someone out here. I want them both arrested. I've already told them they aren't welcome on my land."

The shout caught them both by surprise. Eve twisted to see Connor Evans and Sheriff Larson hiking through the trees toward them. The sheriff looked annoyed, but that expression turned to one of confusion when she saw Eve standing with Atlas.

Eve just felt relief. Lucas might not have been able to call their find in yet, but Connor's constant paranoia about trespassers had done her a favor this time.

Joeseph swore quietly, but it was too late. He was outnumbered now, and unarmed, and Eve suddenly wasn't afraid of him at all. He was a thief and a murderer, and he had just confessed everything to her.

It was time he got what was coming to him.

EPILOGUE

The door to the Granite Mug had a bell over it that jingled whenever Eve entered the building. It was a welcoming sound, but as soon as she heard it each morning, all she could think about was coffee.

Today, her eyes went automatically to the menu the second she was inside. She had tried most of their drinks by now, but they always had a unique flavor each day. Today's flavor was caramel and banana chip.

She wasn't sure how she felt about that, but she was looking forward to finding out.

It wasn't until she joined the line and the person in front of her turned around that she realized he was someone she knew. Aidan looked pleased to see her, a cheerful smile spreading across his face.

"Oh, hey. It's been a while. I think the last time I saw you was on your birthday last week. Alice told me you're a local hero now."

"Ugh, please, don't say anything," she said, moving closer to him so their conversation wouldn't be overheard. "She must have heard about what happened through Sophia. I don't want the whole town hearing about it."

"My lips are sealed." He mimed zipping his lips. "I was actually hoping to run into you so I could ask about something else. Have you heard about the Rock Festival?"

She snorted. "The one interesting thing that happens in Granite each year? I haven't been able to *stop* hearing about it since I moved here."

He grinned. "Me either. I want to go, you know, embrace the whole small-town thing. I still don't know that many people here, and I think it would be a fun way to get a real feel for the town. Do you want to go with me? I thought since we're both newcomers, we could explore the festival together. It might be fun."

It did sound fun, as a matter of fact. The only person Eve really knew in town was Tiana, though Sophia was quickly becoming another friend. She liked what she knew about Aidan, but a handful of conversations each week when they ran into each other at the coffee shop wasn't enough to really get to know someone.

Going to the Rock Festival together would be a fun date. Which was the problem. Eve didn't date, and hadn't for over five years. She had no idea if Aidan was planning on this being a date or not, and asking would make it awkward.

She had a solution, though. "I'm pretty sure Tiana is assuming we'll go together. You could join us, though. Maybe Alice would like to come too. I'd like to get to know her better, especially since she's so close to Sophia. I see her at the horse ranch a lot, helping out, but we're both always so busy we don't have much time to chat."

"That sounds great," he said with enough enthusiasm that she was reassured she wasn't wrecking his idea of a date. "I'll get her on board, and you talk to your friend. We can make a day out of it."

As they shuffled forward in the line, she smiled. Life in Granite wasn't as quiet as she had been expecting … but maybe that wasn't a bad thing.